A MORNING TRUCK RIDE WITH DAD

A series Presented by SharpenYours

Authored and Narrated by Christopher Freeman

Illustrated by Humaima Arts

Edited by Rosalind Cooper

Copyright © 2020 Christopher Freeman.

All rights reserved. No part of this publication may be reproduced or used in any manner without written permission of the copyright owner. Except in the case of brief quotations in a book review. The names, characters, places, and scenarios are either a product of the authors imagination or are used fictitiously.

Dedication/Acknowledgments:

This book is dedicated first and foremost to my parents. Thank you both for your unconditional love and support. And also, to my Paw-Paw, my granddaddy, my uncles, my coaches and my mentors. Thank you all for the positive impact.

To Mama, Aunt Velma, and Aunt DD... I love you all so-much. Y'all are forever my ladies.

A Word from the Author:

"A mother is a child's first love; a father is a child's first hero."

– Chris Freeman

Introduction:

Hey reader, welcome to the first part of the SharpenYours book series. A Morning Truck Ride with Dad is a short story about a father and son who have a strong tie in their relationship. Roland (the father) took it upon himself to lay a strong foundation early on when it came to 13-year-old Nathaniel (the son). Since the day Nate was born, Roland was not only present, but he was highly involved in Nathaniel's life, constantly planting seeds of knowledge, knowing that one day they will blossom into fruits of wisdom. The continuous support, and reassurance of how proud he is of Nate. Expressing his love through discipline, and being an example. My name is Chris Freeman, I am the author and the narrator of this short story. Join the ride with Nate and his father and discover why

this wasn't just an ordinary truck ride.

Story Time

Schools out, and summertime just started! Which is good for Nate, but even better for his father Roland. Spending time with his son was one of his favorite things to do. They did just about anything together, from going fishing at the lake, to playing one on one in the backyard. Nate would even help his dad fix up one of his old cars, a 1996 Chevy Impala. It was a personal project that Roland liked to work on from time to time. However, on this Saturday morning, Nates father decided to take him out for a morning truck ride, to talk, bond, and watch the sunrise. He quietly enters the room as Nate is resting.

Door quietly opens

Walks over to the end of the bed where his bare feet are showing. He goes straight for the big toe and gives it a subtle twist. For some reason, this

always tickled Nate. Roland then says softly,

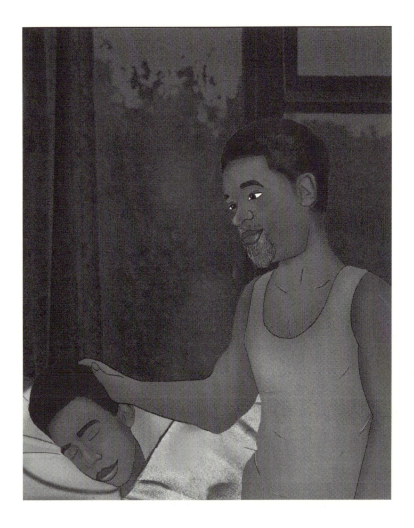

"Hey son. Son, wake up. Put some clothes on, let's go for a ride in the pickup." Nate woke up shocked and in disbelief. The last thing he expected was to be up early on the first day of the summer.

"Dad, come on…. right now? It is five in the morning."

"Yes, right now. Hustle up and get dressed! I'll be in the truck. And don't forget to give your mother a kiss before you head out."

"(sigh) Okay, dad." Nate wasn't much of a morning person; it took him a few moments to get out of bed and wash up. After he was finished getting ready, he headed straight over to his Mother's room. Not concerned about waking her up, he gave her a huge hug and a kiss on the cheek.

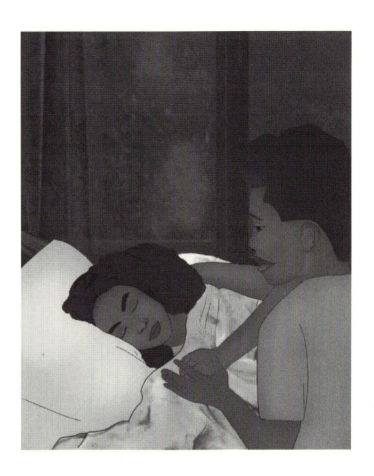

"Mwah! I love you, mommy."

"Aww hey sweetheart, thank you. I love you too, where 'ya headed?"

A MORNING TRUCK RIDE WITH DAD.

"Tuh, I'm not sure ma. Dad just came in the room and said 'get up, let's go for a ride.'" Nate said, as he playfully imitated his father.

"Oh my. Well, y'all be safe and enjoy yourselves, I'll have some breakfast ready when you guys get back. I'll see if your sister wants to help. "

"Okay ma, sounds good!" Roland then honked the horn from outside.

Horn honks

"Well, that's dad outside. I'll see you later, love you!"

As Nate runs off, he gets into his father's truck. As always, he was listening to some instrumental jazz music. He normally listened to this kind of music while he was either getting his day started, studying, or reading.

Truck door opens and closes

"(sighs with intrigue) Who's this, dad?"

"Miles Davis, he was a jazz trumpeter."

"Cool! It sounds good… So where are we going?"

"Nowhere, in particular. I just wanted to get you out of the house, spend some time with you, watch the grand rising of the sun... Do you remember the conversation we had last week at the lake?"

"Yeah! We talked about manhood, and the importance of living a life of high principles, right?"

"Okay, okay, what else did we talk about?"

"We also talked about courage, and that as a man, I have to accept that fear exists. But I must face it at every opportunity because there are lessons and wisdom there. Right?"

"That's good Nathaniel, you got it! I got something else for you. You know I always got something for you." Roland added as he smirked.

"Yeah? What's that, dad? I'm all ears."

"One word – Integrity."

"Integrity? What does that mean?"

"I'm glad you asked. Integrity is a form of honesty. It means doing the right thing in a truthful manner. To take it a step further, it means doing the right thing when nobody is watching. So for instance, you love to play basketball and you love to read books. Which I admire about you by the way. But think about this. Its true – that you attend basketball practice and you put in the necessary work that is expected from your coaches, your teammates, and most importantly, yourself, right? The same thing with school; you do the work; you bring home good grades and you don't get into any trouble. BUT – What are you doing when your coaches aren't around to push you? Or when your teachers not in the classroom to make sure you're staying focused? More specifically, what are you doing in your free time to put yourself in a better position to perform at a higher level in those areas? Integrity is necessary if you have aspirations of making it to the next level, son."

"Wow...You sure do have a way of explaining things, pop. But It sounds like integrity is one of those principles you were telling me about at the lake."

"Aheh, way to connect the dots, Nathaniel. Can you give me an example of integrity?"

"Hmmm... keeping my room clean."

"Great example! The keyword in the statement was *keeping,* because you know that you're supposed to clean your room. But keeping your room clean shows that you have some integrity about you..." Roland suddenly stops in mid-thought, stunned by the beautiful rising of the sun.

"Boy, would you look at that sunrise? Something ain't it?"

"Yeah, it sure is. Hey thanks for bringing out here, dad."

"No problem son, your Paw-Paw used to do this with me all the time. I'm just paying it forward." Roland then pulls over to the side of the road. They hop out and sit on the bed of the truck, to carry on with their conversation.

Truck doors open and close, footsteps in the gravel, the tailgate of the trunk opens

"So, now that summer's here, have you thought about any goals for yourself to achieve by the time school starts back up?"

"Honestly? Not until you explained to me what integrity means."

"Haha that's okay, I have a few for you – just to get you going. Then, you can add more if you want, as they come to mind."

"Goal number one: Exercise Your Mind. Set aside 30 minutes each day to read your favorite book. Now think of reading as a form of 'working out', however not physically, but mentally. Just like you exercise the body, you should also exercise the mind. And an easy way of doing that is by picking up a book and reading. You gotta keep your mind sharp, son."

"Okay." Nathaniel said softly as he nodded.

"The 2nd one I got for you: Work on Your Game... I challenge you to make 300 shots every single day for the entire summer. I don't care where, just get used to scoring the basketball. Remember this, the objective of the game is to score the ball. Master that skill to the best of your ability, and never stop getting better at it.

"And this 3rd one, I want you to keep in your back pocket. Because it's really important that you understand this. Now, whether you succeed or come up short in life, I want you to always take full responsibility for your actions and decisions, or lack thereof, okay? I'm telling you this, not only because I love you, but because you have to be able to handle yourself when your mother and I are not around. Life can be unfair and dangerous at times. And as your father, it is my responsibility to prepare you for it the best way that I can. Because truth be told, you didn't ask to be here. That decision was arranged between me and your mother. So, me not building you up to stand on your own two feet, and one day have a family of your own, would be a disservice to you, and our legacy. You understand?"

"Yes sir…" Nate was at a loss for words, overwhelmed by his father's passion. He felt it. Nate knew that his father loved him, admired him, and wanted the best for him. These are things he needed to hear at the age of 13, and Roland knew that.

"Dad? How do you know all this stuff?"

"Tuh, experience. And not only that, but I always learned something from my experiences. Eventually, you will come to realize that life teaches you the same handful of lessons, just in different scenarios. So for example, there's

- Love
- Understanding
- Sacrifice
- Respect
- Responsibility
- Unselfishness

"But all that will come with time son, just keep living, you'll be fine… Hey I'm getting hungry though, what ya' got a taste for?"

"Pshhh...whatever moms cooking, she said she'll have some breakfast ready for us whenever we get back?"

"God I love that woman! Man! Son? I am one lucky man, because that my friend, is a woman like no other."

"Haha yeah? Why is that? I mean I know she's my mom and all, but what was it about her that let you know she was the one...for you?"

"Mmmm, that's a great question, son... That's honestly a conversation for another time, but I will say this about your mother; It was so much more than just her looks. I mean you have a beautiful mother and all, but she's an incredible woman. And as you continue to grow and mature, you'll start to look for certain characteristics in a woman - beyond her physical appearance. Why do you ask? Is there a girl at school or something?"

"Naw! I mean, yeah kinda...but, I-I was just wondering... I just notice how you look at mom sometimes, and how you treat her, I mean – It's obvious that you love her, and it's always been like that. Even –"

"Hooolddd up! Wait a minute! Time-out! Run that back one more time! Yeah?! Kinda?! Who?! How long?! And before you answer those questions lets hop back in the truck."

Tailgate of the truck closes

"And I want all the details, man."

Footsteps in the gravel, truck doors open and close

"(sigh) Well her name is Stacy. She wrote her number down in my yearbook yesterday on the bus ride home from school. We had 3rd and 4th period together too, so I walked her to class every day. The thing is, I want to call her but - ion wanna say the wrong thing, man. Ya know?"

"I totally understand. Stacy, huh? Well, the fact that you're concerned about saying the wrong thing is just a natural feeling son, so don't pay that any mind – that's normal. It just means you care. But it sounds like she likes you, I mean if she gave you her number on the last day of school, it seems like she wants to keep in touch with you. So, I think, that if you just be yourself, like it sounds like you have been – walking her to class every day, being a perfect gentlemen, I'm sure – then I don't think you'll say the wrong thing to her. I mean you can, but not if you're truly being yourself, ya know?"

"Copy that, lieutenant!" Nathaniel replied as he was smiling and nodding with enthusiasm.

"Hahaha 10-4, soldier! Now let's go eat, huh?!"

"Yeah, I wonder what mama cooked."

"Yeah me too, let's go find out!"

Keys inserted into ignition, truck engine starts and drives off

A MORNING TRUCK RIDE WITH DAD.

Outro:

Hey reader, this concludes the first story of the SharpenYours book series. I hope you enjoyed it! But most importantly I hope that you were able to take something away from it. I look forward to connecting with you all again, as this series continues.

Made in the USA
Middletown, DE
28 June 2022

67794891R00021